# RUSTY THE SQUEAKY ROBOT

*Thank you to my family, my friends and my wife, Dalia.*
*Special thanks to Thomas Forth.*

Quarto is the authority on a wide range of topics.

Quarto educates, entertains and enriches the lives of
our readers—enthusiasts and lovers of hands-on living.

www.quartoknows.com

First Published in 2018 by words & pictures,
an imprint of The Quarto Group.
The Old Brewery, 6 Blundell Street,
London N7 9BH, United Kingdom.
T (0)20 7700 6700 F (0)20 7700 8066
www.QuartoKnows.com

British Library Cataloguing in Publication Data available on request.

ISBN: 978-1-91027-751-5

Manufactured in Dongguan, China TL012018
9 8 7 6 5 4 3 2 1

# RUSTY THE SQUEAKY ROBOT

by Neil Clark

words & pictures

Far, far away, on Planet Robotone,
Rusty the Robot felt sad and alone.

With every nod of his head
and tap of his feet,
he didn't much like
the way he went

SQUEAK!

He squeaked
in the daytime

and squeaked through the night.

He squeaked so much
it gave him a fright!

If he couldn't like his squeak,
then he couldn't like himself.

If only on Planet Robotone
there were robots who could help...

DING! Belle wheeled over.
She was cheery and bright.

"Don't worry, Rusty,
I'll make it all right."

"There's no need to be sad,
all you need is a friend.
Let's go, follow me!
Let's see what's round the bend."

So off they went with
a **DING** and a **SQUEAK**.
I wonder who else Rusty
might meet?

Next they heard a HONK!
Hoot had fun with his sound.

"Don't worry, Rusty, there's no need to feel down."

"Let's all loosen up, have fun and play.
Enjoy yourself, Rusty. It's a much better way!"

So off they all went with
a **HONK, DING** and **SQUEAK.**
Let's see who else
Rusty will meet.

A TWANG announced Twango.

He was ever so smart.

"We all have funny sounds,
but if we add them together...

...we can make brand *new* sounds.
It's really rather clever!"

So off they all went with a
**TWANG, HONK, DING** and **SQUEAK.**
Rusty couldn't wait to see who else
he would meet!

But a **BOOM** interrupted!
The noise shook the ground...

# Look here, it's Boom-Bot!

# He likes to play loud!

BOOM!
BOOM!
BOOM!
BOOM!

Boom-Bot said "Yo!" and pumped out a beat.
So the robots all moved and tapped their feet.

Soon they were dancing, and Rusty was too.
Their sounds mixed together and
made a great robot tune!

# BOOM-BOOM, HONK-HONK,
# TWANG, DING-DING.

Rusty said, "I'm no longer worried about a thing!"

"It's OK to be different. It's OK to be me."

"My sound makes me special.

That's how we should all be."

And so with a nod, tap, skip and a leap,

Rusty said, "Now I love the way I go...